23 JUL 2019

Delete

THE LONDON BOROUGH
www.bromley.gov.uk

Renewals

0333 370 4700

Please
by th arena.yourlondonlibrary.net/
Books m web/bromley
phone and Internet.

AUTHOR: Tom Easton

Dedicated to Theo and Tilly, who helped

put Hypnoscam together

ORCHARD BOOKS
Carmelite House
50 Victoria Embankment
London EC4Y 0DZ

First published by Orchard Books in 2017

HASBRO and its logo, TRANSFORMERS, TRANSFORMERS ROBOTS IN
DISGUISE, the logo and all related characters are
trademarks of Hasbro and are used with permission.

A CIP catalogue record for this book is available
from the British Library.

ISBN 978 1 40834 498 9

1 3 5 7 9 10 8 6 4 2

Printed in Great Britain

Orchard Books
An imprint of Hachette Children's Group
Part of The Watts Publishing Group Limited
An Hachette UK Company
www.hachette.co.uk

MIX
Paper from
responsible sources
FSC® C104740

The paper and board used in this book are made from wood from
responsible sources.

DINOBOT
DISASTER

BY TOM EASTON

ORCHARD

MEET THE TEAM:

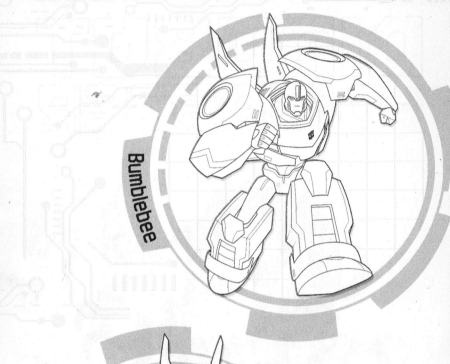

Bumblebee

Sideswipe

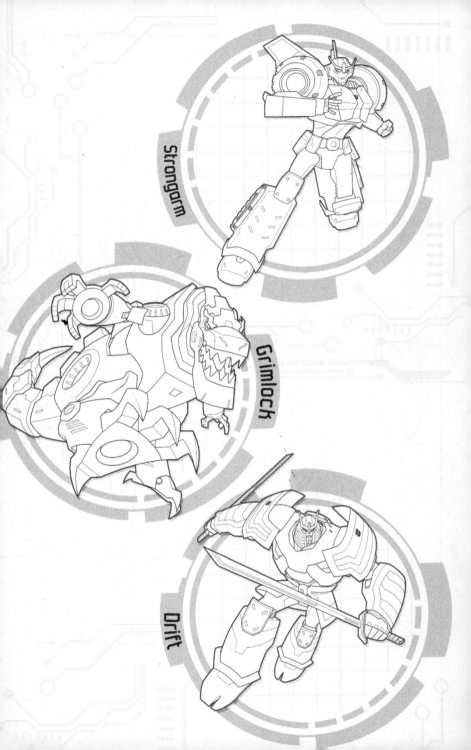

Strongarm

Grimlock

Drift

CONTENTS

FLICK TO SCROLL

STATUS REPORT: A prison ship from the planet Cybertron has crashed on Earth, and deadly robot criminals – the Decepticons – have escaped.

It's up to a team of Autobots to find them and get them back into stasis. Lieutenant Bumblebee, rebellious Sideswipe and police trainee Strongarm have taken the Groundbridge from Cybertron to Earth to track them down.

Along with bounty hunter, Drift, reformed Decepticon, Grimlock, and the malfunctioning pilot of the ship, Fixit, as well as the two humans who own the scrapyard where the ship crashed, Russell Clay and his dad, Denny, the robots in disguise must find the Decepticons, before they destroy the entire world ...

CHAPTER ONE

GRIMLOCK BASHED THE ENEMY BOT.
SMASH! It flew away and bounced off
the wall of the control room, landing in a
crumpled heap. A second bot charged at
him. He waited for the right moment
then flipped his huge tail around in a
great arc, slapping the enemy away. It
sailed into a bank of computers, landing
with a flash of sparks and a crackle of
energy.

But there were more enemy bots all
around. Small and grey with vicious
weapons clustered all over them, they
raced towards Grimlock from every
direction. The Dinobot stood tall and

roared, ready for the battle. Suddenly one of the bots made a piercing, high-pitched wailing sound. Grimlock blinked at it in surprise as it started talking to him ...

"... Autobots! Action Stations! Alan ... Albert ... ALERT!"

Grimlock woke up on top of a huge pile of old, dented cars, trying to work out what was happening. Gradually he realised it wasn't an enemy bot talking to him! It was Fixit. He'd been dreaming about smashing bots and now he was awake. He sat up and peered over the side of the pile.

Woken by Fixit's cries, the other Autobots sprang into action as well. First came Bumblebee, the leader, a yellow sports car, flashing across the scrapyard, heading for the command centre.

Strongarm, in the form of a police car, roared out of her bay. Next, racing from his garage, came the sleek red racing car that was the vehicle form of Sideswipe.

The three Autobots screeched to a halt outside the control room and with a click and a clack transformed into three powerful bots. Bumblebee looked around. "Where's Grimlock hiding?" he said.

"Right here, boss," Grimlock replied from the top of his towering pile of scrap cars. He leapt into the air and sent the other bots scattering as he landed with a huge thud that shook the whole scrapyard. Grimlock was in his dinosaur form. He roared, his great metal teeth glinting menacingly in the lights of the command centre.

"Hiding isn't Grimlock's strong suit," Sideswipe said.

"You won't find me hiding when there are bots to be smashed," Grimlock replied.

"Come on," Bumblebee said. "Let's find out what this alert is all about."

The Autobots had come to Earth on a secret mission. Their job was to find and capture Decepticons who had escaped from the Alchemor – a prison spaceship which had crashed on Earth, scattering two hundred stasis pods. Each stasis pod contained an evil Decepticon. And now it looked like they'd detected another one on the loose!

Grimlock waited outside the command centre as the others went in. He was a

bit too big to fit inside. He was different
to the others. He was the biggest
and baddest Dinobot around. Actually,
he was the only Dinobot around.

Grimlock had been a Decepticon prisoner on board the Alchemor. He'd been arrested for smashing things up. He wasn't really bad though, he just sometimes got carried away. And when the Autobots had found him, he'd joined their team. His proudest day was when he was allowed to replace his Decepticon badge with an Autobot one. Grimlock liked his new team but sometimes he found it hard to fit in. Not being able to transform into a vehicle made it hard to disguise himself when there were humans around. And he was just the worst at hide-and-seek.

Denny and Russell, their human friends, came running over from the trailer they lived in. Denny was the owner of the scrapyard and Russell was his son. They helped hide the Autobots and make sure they weren't seen by other humans.

"What is it, Fixit?" Bumblebee asked. Fixit was a small bot who looked a bit like a cement mixer. He had been the pilot of the Alchemor, and since the crash Fixit's language processor sometimes malfunctioned and he got his words wrong.

"It's a weed ... wheel ... weak signal, but it could be a Decepticon," Fixit said, pointing to a fuzzy blob on the scanner screen.

"Interesting," Bumblebee said, peering

at it. "It looks like it's right in the middle of Crown City."

"Or," Fixit went on, "it might just be an insect on the radar dish."

"You woke us all up just to squash a bug?" Sideswipe grumbled.

"It might be a bug," Bumblebee said. "But it might be a Decepticon. Fixit did the right thing by waking us. The Primes gave us the job of protecting the people of Earth by catching every last Decepticon and putting them back into stasis. Even just one of them loose can destroy an entire city."

"Bumblebee's right," Strongarm said. "And who wants to waste time sleeping when there might be Decepticons to catch and lock up?"

"You mean Decepticons to SMASH!" Grimlock roared from outside. "I'm ready. Let's roll!"

"Not tonight, Grimlock," Bumblebee said as the Autobot joined him outside. "You'll have to stay behind. We can't risk letting you be seen. I'm afraid a Dinobot rampaging through the streets of Crown City would be just too conspicuous."

"That's not fair," Grimlock said as disappointment swept through his processors.

"Hey, count yourself lucky," yawned Sideswipe. "You get to stay and catch up on your beauty sleep. Looks like you could do with it."

Grimlock growled and swung his huge, clanking tail around, taking Sideswipe's feet out from under him. Sideswipe slammed into the ground in a cloud of dust.

"That's enough, you two," said Bumblebee. "We have a job to do. Autobots, rev up and roll!"

Grimlock watched sadly as the three bots transformed back into vehicle form. Engines roaring, they raced across the scrapyard and out through the gate, their rear lights shining brightly. They skidded hard on to the road and disappeared in the direction of Crown City.

"Never mind, Grimlock," Rusty said, patting the huge bot on his leg. "There'll be more Decepticons to fight tomorrow. Get some sleep."

Denny was already yawning as he and
Rusty walked back towards the trailer.
"Good night, Grimlock," he called sleepily.

Grimlock climbed slowly back up to the top of his tower. He sat grumpily for a while. It wasn't fair. It wasn't his fault he was different to the others, it was just the way he was built. He closed his eyes, trying to get back to sleep. That had been such a good dream, smashing those enemy bots like that. Sometimes Grimlock missed the old days when he didn't have to worry about being seen, or remember whose side he was on. And he could just SMASH, BASH and CRASH enemies from morning until night. He knew that he'd often been smashing the wrong bots back then, but he'd never had to hide himself away, and at least he'd been able to get a good night's sleep afterwards.

He tossed and turned for a while, wondering what the others were up to right now. Maybe Bumblebee had made a mistake. Maybe they were in trouble and needed him to come and smash some Decepticons and help them escape ...!

Suddenly, Grimlock heard something off in the woods that surrounded the scrapyard. A sort of WHUMPING sound, but muffled, and distant. What was that? Had he imagined it?

But no, there it was again. WHUMP WHUMP WHUMP. Grimlock sat up, peering into the distance. Did he see a light? He leapt off the car tower, wondering if he should wake Denny and Rusty. But no, it might be nothing. There weren't likely to be any humans in the woods, not at this time of night. He could go without anyone seeing him.

Again he heard the sound, his sensitive ear sensors picking up the distinctive noise again. That settled it! Grimlock set off, lumbering through the trees. He could be surprisingly quick when he needed to be, but it was tricky threading through the tree trunks. In the old days he would have just smashed them aside but Denny had explained to him about protecting nature and Rusty had explained about not announcing your presence, especially when playing hide-and-seek.

Grimlock walked for ages through the dark woods until he reached a part of the woods he'd never been to before.

He nearly gave up a couple of times and turned back, only for the sound to appear again, urging him on. After he'd walked for a couple of miles, he realised the sound was getting closer. He slowed down, trying to be as quiet as a Dinobot could be.

Grimlock came to a deep valley and stopped to listen. He could hear a stream at the bottom, he could hear the wind through the trees ... and then he heard the WHUMP WHUMP WHUMP sound again. But this time it was accompanied by a light.

There was something down there in that valley.

Grimlock felt his excitement build. It could be an escaped Decepticon ...

Maybe he'd get to do some smashing tonight after all! Grimlock was about to rush into the valley, but then he paused. Should he go back and wait for Bumblebee and the others? But if he did that, the Decepticon might escape.

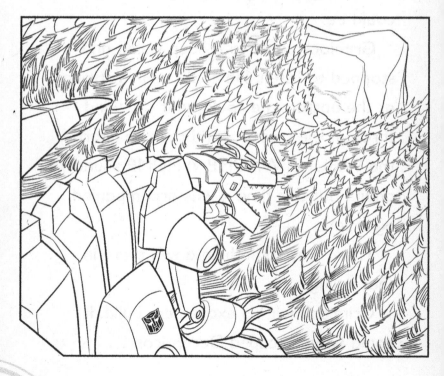

Grimlock shook his head. This was simple: if there was a bad bot down there, he needed to go and smash it.

And smash it HARD.

CHAPTER TWO

GRIMLOCK CHARGED DOWN THE slope. Too late he remembered what Rusty had told him about being sneaky. But there was no point trying to be quiet now. He smashed trees aside as he charged and, unable to help himself, let out a huge roar. ROOOOAAAARR! Grimlock reached the bottom of the valley and crashed through a the trees right into a clearing, lit by the moon.

In the centre of the clearing stood a bot. A slim, green bot with two large spotlights on his chest. Between the bright spotlights, Grimlock saw the badge of the Decepticons! Grimlock roared with delight. Finally, something to smash! He was just about to charge, when he remembered something Strongarm had said about following the rules.

"Err, OK," Grimlock said, trying to remember how it worked. Usually Bumblebee or Strongarm did this bit. "I'm an Autobot. You're a Decepticon. So you have to come with me."

"Why?" the Decepticon replied.

"Err," Grimlock said. "So I can put you into a stasis pod."

"I don't want to go into a stasis pod," the Decepticon said calmly.

"Good," Grimlock said, relieved. "I was hoping you'd say that. That means I get to SMASH you."

Usually, when Grimlock said things like

that, the bot he was talking to would look scared and try to run away. But not this time. The Decepticon just took out a long blade and stood there, twirling it quickly before him. Grimlock heard the blade hum as it whipped through the air, spinning so fast it became a blur.

Grimlock shrugged. A puny sword wouldn't even scratch his thick metal plating. He lowered his head and charged towards the Decepticon, powerful hind legs forcing him on, ready to smash.

The Decepticon stood still, making no effort to get out of the way. Grimlock carried on and ploughed right into the enemy bot, braced for the impact …

… except there was no impact. Instead, Grimlock just went right through the

Decepticon and out the other side. Astonished and unable to stop, Grimlock went on and hit the cliff wall on the other side of the clearing with a great crash. He turned around, his head spinning.

Then a big rock broke off the cliff wall and clonked him on his head.

"Ow!" Grimlock roared. "How did you do that?" He wobbled unsteadily and peered towards the two bots in the clearing ...

Wait. Two bots?

Grimlock counted again. *One ... two.* Yes, there were definitely two now. Both the same, each with a great whirling blade.

"One, two, it doesn't matter," he growled. "I'll fight a whole army of you if

I have to." He lowered his head and prepared to charge forward again as the two Decepticons whirled their blades. Something about the way the spinning blades made a pattern made Grimlock's head go a bit fuzzy, but he shook his head and charged.

Once again Grimlock lumbered across the clearing, once again he ploughed into the bot and once again he went straight through, as though the Decepticon was made of smoke. He carried on and this time crashed into a thicket of trees, smashing them to one side. He stumbled and came to rest in a heap of tangled limbs and massive tree trunks. What was going on?

He threw the tree trunks aside and

clambered to his feet again. This time, when he turned, there were even more Decepticons. He tried to count them again. "One, two, three ..." Grimlock forgot what came after three, but there was definitely another one as well as the three that he could count. They were all identical.

"Who ARE you guys?" he called.

One of the bots bowed his head in a grand gesture. "My name is Hypnoscam," he said, smoothly.

"And aren't you going to introduce me to your friends?" Grimlock asked. "I didn't learn much at school, but I do know my manners."

"Why don't you come and meet them in person?" Hypnoscam suggested.

Grimlock moved forward, more cautiously this time. His processors whirred hotly as he tried to work out what was happening. He moved closer to one of the Decepticons who stood waiting, whirling his sword blade. The lights on the bot's chest glowed brightly.

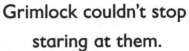

Grimlock couldn't stop staring at them.

"I don't think you're real ..." Grimlock said. "I think you're like ... a bug on a radar dish."

Suddenly the Decepticon struck with his twirling sword blade, cracking it sharply against Grimlock's chest. Grimlock fell back on to his tail in surprise. That hurt!

"That real enough for you?" The Decepticon laughed.

With a roar Grimlock leaned forward, twisted his great body and swung his tail, whipping it around with a loud snap.

It made solid contact with the smaller bot, who went flying across the clearing, landing amongst the trees with a great crash.

"If you can hit, then you can get hit," Grimlock growled in satisfaction. But then he suddenly found himself surrounded by three more Decepticons, all identical to the first. They began slicing and cutting with their long swords. Grimlock tried to defend himself against the blows but there were just too many Hypnoscams to tackle. He swept his tail again and again, knocking his attackers aside, only for more to appear from nowhere.

At a shouted command from somewhere, half a dozen Hypnoscams leapt into the air and transformed into the shape of a military helicopter. The swords the bot-forms used were now the helicopters' rotor blades. They spun around, blurry and hypnotic. Grimlock looked away as the lights blinded him. Now he was being attacked from the air as well as the ground. He roared and attacked with arms, teeth and tail, but he could feel his power gradually draining. The Hypnoscams darted in one or two at a time, thrusting or slashing with their swords, dealing him minor damage each time. He knocked as many away into the trees as he could, but there were always more who'd break through his defences and hit him from behind, or from overhead.

Grimlock roared as more and more copies of Hypnoscam piled on top of him. Each one was small and easily beaten on its own, but with so many, how could he ever fight them all?

CHAPTER THREE

GRIMLOCK WAS GETTING MORE
and more tired as he battled one
Hypnoscam, then another. His enemies'
eyes glowed brightly, dazzling him as
he swung and chomped. Each of the
bots seemed completely real – their
swords certainly hurt, and when he hit
them they were solid, hard metal, but
he noticed that if he smashed one
away into the woods it would just
disappear, blade, lights and all.
Hypnoscam was playing tricks on his
brain!

Then, as Grimlock pounded one of
the bots into the ground at his feet,

something odd happened. Grimlock had an idea. All these bots were just copies, but they must be copies of something, right? So what, or who, were they copies of?

There must be an original Hypnoscam, the real one. He just had to figure out which one it was.

Grimlock spun round fast, his tail

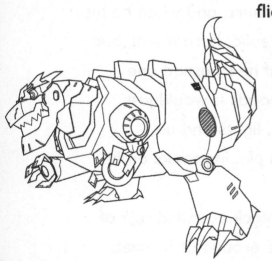 flicking though the air. He ignored a series of hard blows against his back as he scanned the army of bots attacking him.

And then he saw it. One of the Hypnoscams looked different to the others. He seemed more solid, denser. He stood away from the battle, watching, whirling his long blade. His big round spotlight eyes glowed with a strange intensity and seemed to spin.

That's the real Hypnoscam. Now all I need to do is ...

Grimlock forgot about all the other Hypnoscams surrounding him. The blows on his back stopped hurting. He was transfixed by the lights, and by the whirling blade, shimmering in the moonlight.

Hypnoscam clicked his fingers and all the copies disappeared, leaving just one Dinobot and one Decepticon.

Somewhere, deep inside in Grimlock's processors, he knew that he could win this fight. That there was really only one enemy, and he was right in front of him. All he had to do was lower his head and charge.

But he couldn't bring himself to do it. For all his strength and power. Grimlock was helpless. He was completely under the control of the Decepticon.

"Well," Hypnoscam said, stepping forward. "That was easier than I'd thought it would be." He peered into Grimlock's eyes. "How lucky for me that you should stumble into my lair," the Decepticon said. "A powerful Dinobot with a tiny brain. Just what I was looking for."

Grimlock tried to roar, but found himself unable to speak.

Hypnoscam laughed. "I can make you do anything I want."

Grimlock felt a surge of frustration mixed with anger. He tried to move again, but couldn't.

"And what I want," Hypnoscam went on, "is to destroy Crown City, once and for all."

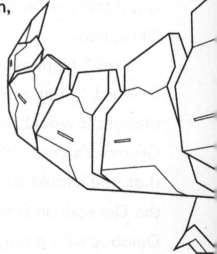

CHAPTER FOUR

"GRIMLOCK!" BUMBLEBEE SHOUTED. Dawn had broken over the scrapyard

"We don't have time for hide-and-seek!" Strongarm called, peering around a pile of old washing machines.

"Where has he gone?" Sideswipe said. "Did he say he was going somewhere, Denny?"

Denny shook his head. "No, in fact he was supposed to help me chomp down a shipment of old cars into scrap metal this morning. He said he was looking forward to it because he was so hungry."

At that moment, the door to the mobile home was flung back and Rusty came sprinting out, holding a portable vid-screen. "Guys, guys," he cried. "You gotta see this!"

"What is it?" Bumblebee asked, striding forward.

"I was flying my drone around the woods," Rusty said, "and I found Grimlock."

"That's great," Bumblebee said.

"You might not say that when you see what he's doing," Rusty said, holding out the screen. The Autobots clustered around to see.

Bumblebee groaned.

Grimlock was on the rampage. He was lumbering through the trees, roaring, smashing them aside, leaving a trail of destruction behind him. Overhead flew a

military helicopter, keeping pace but
making no attempt to stop the Dinobot.

"He's headed straight for Crown City,"
Strongarm said.

"What is he doing?"
Sideswipe said. "Has
he turned back into a
Decepticon?"

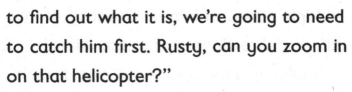

"I'm sure there's a
good explanation,"
Bumblebee said. "But
to find out what it is, we're going to need
to catch him first. Rusty, can you zoom in
on that helicopter?"

Rusty tweaked the drone controls and
the helicopter suddenly loomed huge on
the screen. As it swam into focus, the
Autobots gasped. On the side of the

helicopter they could see a familiar symbol.

"It's a Decepticon!" Strongarm said.

"His name is Hypnoscam," Fixit said, behind them. "I looked him up on the manifest from the Alchemor."

"Tell us what you know about this Hypnoscam," Bumblebee said.

"He is a slippery cucumber … custard pie … customer," Fixit said. "Not very strong, but he has the ability to make multiple copies of himself to attack from different directions at the same time."

"Multiple copies of a weak bot doesn't sound too terrifying," Sideswipe said. "Let's get out there, grab him and get Grimlock back here before any humans can spot him."

"Not so fast," Fixit said. "Hypnoscam doesn't just have the ability to make copies of himself. He can also make copies of any bot he has managed to hypnotise."

As one, the team looked back at the screen, where Grimlock continued smashing his way through the forest, still followed by Hypnoscam. Denny swallowed nervously. "Lots of ... Grimlocks?" he said. "But Grimlock is huge. He's one of the biggest and strongest there is. If Hypnoscam makes multiple copies of him, then Crown City will be flattened."

"How did that Dino-dummy get himself into this ..." Sideswipe began, but was cut off by Bumblebee.

"That's enough," the Autobot said.

"Grimlock is a vital member of our team. And he's our friend. He needs our help, not our mockery."

"Well then," Strongarm said. "What are we waiting for? Let's go and get him."

Bumblebee looked at Sideswipe, who nodded. "Yeah, let's go and get him," she said. "And let's smash that sneaky Decepticon while we're at it."

Bumblebee nodded. "OK, Autobots, let's rev up and roll out." They transformed into vehicle form, Denny and Rusty jumping into Strongarm's cab, ready to find their friend.

But as they raced out of the scrapyard, engines roaring, Bumblebee was worried. Sideswipe had been right when he'd pointed out that Grimlock was the biggest and strongest of them all. If Hypnoscam made multiple copies of Grimlock there was no way his team could overcome them.

It was a Dinobot disaster.

CHAPTER FIVE

EVEN WITHOUT RUSTY'S DRONE IT wouldn't have been difficult to locate Grimlock. As the Autobots raced through the outskirts of Crown City, they saw cars overturned, lamp-posts twisted and power lines brought down. Grimlock had left a trail of destruction behind him.

"Luckily it's still early and there aren't many people around," Denny pointed out over the radio.

"We have to stop him before he gets to the city centre," Bumblebee said, his voice crackling across the radio waves. "There'll be many more people there, and if Grimlock starts smashing buildings there could be casualties."

The Autobots revved their engines and roared through the quiet city streets.

"He's just knocked over an ice-cream truck," Rusty said, reporting what he could see from the drone. "Now he's eating the giant plastic cone on the top. I don't think he likes it much. Now he's heading for a doughnut factory. He must be hungry."

"I've got plenty of junk back at the scrapyard," Denny said, shaking his head in annoyance. "He can eat that."

"I can see Hypnoscam!" Strongarm cried. "Dead ahead."

Bumblebee turned his wheels and skidded sharply around a corner, turning in the direction of the hovering helicopter.

The others followed and in less than a minute they raced into a wide junction where they saw Grimlock standing by a red-brick building, a huge, illuminated doughnut half-eaten in his great jaws.

Grimlock turned as they screeched to a stop before him.

"Grimlock!" Bumblebee cried as he transformed back into a bot. Usually he wouldn't transform out of his vehicle form where there might be humans, but there was no one around just now. "Denny, Rusty," Bumblebee called. "Keep an eye on Hypnoscam while we deal with Grimlock."

Denny and Rusty leapt out of Strongarm's cab and she too transformed, followed by Sideswipe.

Grimlock ignored them and got back to eating his snack.

"Grimlock," Strongarm shouted, using her loudspeaker. "Drop the doughnut and put your digits in the air!"

Grimlock spun, roared and hurled the half-doughnut right at her. The heavy plastic object caught her full in the chest and sent her clattering and sliding across the junction until she came to a stop against the wall of a shopfront on the opposite side. She looked up and groaned. "I guess he's not going to come quietly then," she said.

"He did drop the doughnut, at least," Sideswipe said. "But don't worry. I got this." He rushed at Grimlock, but the Dinobot just flicked his tail and smacked

Sideswipe away into the air. He sailed in a low arc and smashed through a plate-glass shopfront, landing amongst a pile of toys. A xylophone fell from a shelf and landed on his head with a tuneless tinkle.

"Ouch," Sideswipe groaned.

"Now come on, Grimlock," Bumblebee said, approaching the Dinobot slowly, an arm stretched out in friendship. "Do you recognise us? We're your friends."

Grimlock stared at him, his head to one side, as if he was thinking, trying to remember.

"That's it," Bumblebee said, with a friendly smile. "I'm Bumblebee. Remember me?"

For a moment, Grimlock seemed to recognise Bumblebee. He nodded, but then Bumblebee heard Denny's voice crackling through the loudspeaker.

"Hypnoscam is approaching!"

Grimlock suddenly stood tall and roared. Then he dropped his head and charged at Bumblebee.

"NOOOOO," Bumblebee cried just before the huge bulk of the Dinobot smashed into him. He pinged off the tough armour of Grimlock's head and went flying, landing in in a burger joint, covered in ketchup.

Bumblebee stood. "Right," he said. "That's it. Time to go up a gear. He can't fight all three of us at once. Autobots, attack!"

From three different directions, the three Autobots raced towards the Dinobot, hoping to overpower him through strength in numbers. But as they ran, something strange happened. A shimmer to the left of Grimlock turned into something solid. A second Dinobot, identical to him. Then a second shimmer on the other side became a third. The three Dinobots each turned to face one of the Autobots.

"What's going on?" Sideswipe cried.

"Remember what Fixit said," Rusty cried. "Hypnoscam can't just make copies of himself. He can make copies of those he's controlling too."

"Just our luck he happens to be controlling the biggest and baddest bot around," Sideswipe said.

Undeterred, Bumblebee carried on towards the Grimlock in the middle. Grimlock was big and strong, but Bumblebee was no pushover. He ducked under a lunge from Grimlock's chomping jaws and punched with an uppercut, setting Grimlock back on to his tail.

Strongarm knew some moves too. All of them in fact: she spent hours at night reading through hand-to-hand combat manuals and was familiar with at least a dozen approved forms of martial arts from the furthest reaches of Cybertron.

The key to defeating a heavier, stronger opponent, she thought as she leapt over Grimlock's sweeping tail, *is to be patient and use their strength against them.* Strongarm dodged two blows from Grimlock's forearms and waited. Grimlock roared in anger and charged forward. At the last minute she dived to one side and rolled clear. Grimlock carried on charging, slamming head-first into the grille of a parked truck and leaving a massive dent.

Meanwhile, Sideswipe darted in close to his opponent, without waiting, and unleashed a furious series of blows, driving the surprised Grimlock back. With a whoop, Sideswipe leapt feet-first and kicked Grimlock's chest hard.

Grimlock fell back with a grunt.

"YES!" Sideswipe whooped, and turned around.

"NO!" he cried.

Because behind him stood more Grimlocks. Six of them.

Sideswipe's eyes went wide as the six Dinobots lowered their heads and charged. He turned to run, but too late, and found himself trampled into the tarmac. He raised his head, circuits spinning in a haze. "This is turning into a real street fight."

Strongarm helped him to his feet as Bumblebee came over to join them. All three Autobots looked battered and bruised. They stood back-to back. The multiple Grimlocks circled them, roaring.

"We'll never defeat them all," Strongarm said.

"Not by fighting," Bumblebee said. "But we've got something more effective."

"Please tell me it's an even bigger Dinobot," Sideswipe said. "In fact, I'll take six of them."

"It's not a bot, or a weapon,"
Bumblebee said as the Dinobots closed in
on them. "We have to make Grimlock
remember us. Make him remember we're
a team and that we're his friends."

"He's not being very friendly at the
moment," Sideswipe muttered.

Bumblebee ignored him and looked
closely at each of the Dinobots in turn.
"There," he said, pointing. "That's our
Grimlock." The others looked at the
Dinobot he was indicating. There was
something different about him. He
seemed more solid, more ... real.

Bumblebee stepped forward and held
out his hands. The Dinobot stalked
forward and opened his great jaws wide.

His eyes flashed with fury.

"Grimlock," Bumblebee said. "Just wait, before you attack. Let me say something." Bumblebee looked into his friend's eyes, trying to get through to the real Grimlock somewhere inside. Grimlock paused and, encouraged, Bumblebee continued.

"I just wanted to say ... sorry,"

"Sorry?" Sideswipe muttered behind him. "He's the one who should say sorry. I think he's cracked my chassis."

Bumblebee ignored Sideswipe and fixed Grimlock's gaze. "I'm ... *we're* sorry for leaving you behind at the scrapyard. That was wrong. We should have taken you with us. You're part of the team and, more importantly, you're our friend."

As he said this, Grimlock stared hard
at him, watching. There was a pause
when Bumblebee had finished speaking.
Then Grimlock shook his head. "Boss?"
the Dinobot said. "What's going on?

I remember a forest, and a whirling circle, and a whumping sound ..."
Grimlock looked around and saw the other Grimlocks, then up at the hovering Hypnoscam.

"DECEPTICON!" he roared.

Grimlock spun, whipping his heavy tail around like a baseball bat. He knocked the nearest copy of himself up high into the air right towards the helicopter, scoring a perfect hit.

"STEEEE-RRIIIKE!" Rusty cried.

Hypnoscam's blades crunched into the heavy Dinobot copy and the helicopter lurched crazily as it turned to flee. It flew a for a few seconds, before falling from the sky, demolishing a fish restaurant a couple of blocks away. Instantly, the other copies of Grimlock disappeared as Hypnoscam's power was broken.

"Get that Decepticon!" Bumblebee ordered. Strongarm and Sideswipe transformed into vehicle form and raced towards the crash site, their tyres screeching.

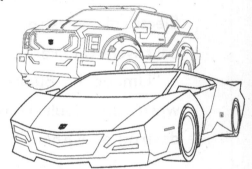

"Nice to have you back, Grim," Bumblebee said.

"Nice to be back," Grimlock replied. Then he scratched his head. "Though I'm not really sure where I went."

"I meant what I said," Bumblebee went on. "About being sorry. I shouldn't have left you behind."

"Well, I'm sorry for going off on my own," Grimlock replied. He looked around at the trail of destruction. Fire hydrants sprayed water high into the air. Electrical cables spat and sparked. Three cars were on fire. "Did I do all this?"

"Um, yeah," Bumblebee said. "But it wasn't your fault. Hypnoscam made you destroy everything."

"You know, I used to think that nothing was better than smashing things up," Grimlock said. "But that was before I found my new team."

The Autobots were interrupted by the sound of rotor blades. They spun to see that Hypnoscam had managed to get airborne again and was racing off into the cloudy skies. Soon after, Sideswipe

and Strongarm
returned.

"Sorry, Boss,"
Strongarm said.
"He escaped."

"Don't
worry,"
Bumblebee said.
"He won't get
away for long.

And we have a nice cosy stasis pod
waiting for him."

Sirens wailed in the distance, coming
towards them.

"For now, though," Bumblebee said,
"let's get back to the scrapyard. We'll
have to leave all this mess for the humans
to clear up."

Grimlock hopped on to Strongarm's trailer and Bumblebee and Sideswipe hastily covered him with a tarpaulin. Bumblebee was about to transform back into vehicle form when he noticed something shimmering in a nearby pool of water from the fire hydrant. He'd seen that sort of rippling before and knew exactly what it meant.

Bumblebee rushed over to the pool and peered into it. The shimmering formed itself into a familiar image which spoke to him.

"Bumblebee, are you there? ... Bumblebee, do you read me?"

"Optimus!" Bumblebee cried. "Yes, I'm here. I mean ... I read you. It's great to hear your voice."

"You might not think it so great when you hear what I have to say," Optimus Prime replied. He looked grave. "I'm afraid I have bad news."

CHAPTER SIX

BACK AT THE SCRAPYARD,
Sideswipe, Strongarm, Denny and Rusty
paced outside the command centre while
Bumblebee talked to Optimus through
the reflection on a shiny metal screen
that Fixit had hastily set up.

Grimlock climbed back up his tower of
cars and sat there sadly, thinking over
what he'd done.

"Here in the realm of the Primes,"
Optimus was saying, "news of Grimlock's
betrayal has reached the oldest and
most powerful Autobots – the Thirteen.
Some of them never trusted that a
Dinobot could be a loyal member of
the Autobot team."

"It wasn't a betrayal," Bumblebee pointed out. "Grimlock was hypnotised by a Decepticon. Hypnoscam is the real enemy."

"Grimlock caused a lot of damage," Optimus said.

"It wasn't his fault!" Rusty cried.

"Legally, he is responsible," Strongarm butted in. "According to the rulebook, that is."

Optimus went on. "There are some who remain unconvinced that Grimlock is a genuine convert to the Autobots."

"Grimlock is as committed to the Autobot cause as I am," Bumblebee replied, angrily.

"I know that is true," Optimus replied. "But some of the Primes have doubts,

and one of them in particular, Liege
Maximo, has taken this opportunity to
cause trouble for me ... and for you."

"What sort of trouble?" Sideswipe
asked.

"Liege Maximo has declared that
Grimlock has had his last chance – he
must pay for the damage he's done and
be sentenced like any other Decepticon
criminal. His punishment is to be put back
in stasis."

"NO!" Rusty cried.

"Come on, Rusty," Denny said, pulling
his son away gently. "This is a matter for
the Autobots to sort out."

"I can't do it," Bumblebee said.
"Grimlock is the strongest of us all. We
need him if we want to have any chance

of completing our task here."

"I'm sorry," Optimus said. "But you have no choice. I order you to put Grimlock back into stasis."

"Is there anything in the law books that can help us?" Sideswipe asked Strongarm. "Can we fight this?"

Strongarm shook her head. "The Primes ARE the law. Once they have decided on something, that's it."

"Bumblebee?" Optimus said, filling the screen. "I'll need proof that this has been done. It's the only way I'll be able to satisfy Liege Maximo and the other Primes that justice has been served."

"Justice ...?" Bumblebee said. "This isn't justice."

"Yes, it is," a deep voice said behind

them. They turned to see Grimlock
standing there, his tail trailing in the dust.
"I smashed up the city. I accept the
punishment. I'll put myself back in stasis."

"Thank you, Grimlock," Optimus said. "I can't promise anything, but I will insist we review your case at the next meeting of the Primes."

Grimlock nodded, then turned and walked to the shed where his old stasis chamber was stored. The Autobots followed him. Fixit was recording everything on his inbuilt camera to send back to the Primes.

"We'll do everything we can," Bumblebee said. He couldn't believe this was happening.

"I'll look through the book of Prime Law straight away," Strongarm said, "to see if I can find anything that might help your appeal." Grimlock pressed a series of buttons on the outside of the stasis pod to begin the hibernation procedure.

"I've been in stasis before," he said. "It's not so bad. I'll dream about smashing bad bots."

Sideswipe had been quiet up until now, but now he stepped forward and spoke. "I don't want you to go," he said. "I know we fight sometimes. But at the end of the day, you're my friend."

"Thanks, buddy," Grimlock replied as the stasis chamber door began to close slowly. Steam billowed around him. "I'll miss you too, but at least now I'll catch up on my beauty sleep."

He winked, then the door was closed. The status lights on the outside of the pod went green, indicating that the hibernation procedure was complete.

"Video uprooted ... uplooted ... uploaded," Fixit said as he fired the video of Grimlock's imprisonment to the realm of the Primes.

"Great," Sideswipe said immediately. "Now we've proved that we've locked him up, we can let him straight back out again."

"You know we can't do that," Bumblebee sighed.

"Why not?" Sideswipe said. "The Primes don't have to know."

"We have to abide by the law, otherwise we're no better than the Decepticons," Strongarm said.

"Speak for yourself," Sideswipe said. "I know right from wrong, and it has nothing to do with the law."

"I order you not to touch that stasis pod," Bumblebee said. "We'll wait for the appeal. Right now, there's nothing more we can do."

CHAPTER SEVEN

GRIMLOCK STOOD UNCERTAINLY AS a hundred Hypnoscams rushed at him. He smashed the first one aside, then the second, and the third. But then he was swamped by the smaller bots, knocking him down under their combined weight. He roared and thrust himself up on his powerful hind legs, tossing the smaller bots aside like rag dolls.

He swept his tail, smashing half a dozen bots away, sending them sailing across the room to slam against a smooth white wall. But then the Hypnoscams changed tactics. They started throwing doughnuts at him.

Grimlock, who was feeling very hungry, tried to catch them in his jaws as they flew at him but frustratingly, they seemed to disappear into thin air as he chomped on them.

Then something even stranger happened. The wall opened up with a hiss and a puff of smoke. The Hypnoscams evaporated into thin air. Grimlock blinked, trying to work out what was going on. He stepped forward and peered out through the hole. There was someone there: a bot. Blue and white.

"Strongarm?" he said.

"What are you waiting for?" Strongarm hissed. "An invitation?"

Grimlock lumbered forward, still trying to puzzle it out. "Is my sentence over already?" he asked.

"Not technically," Strongarm whispered. "They haven't had the appeal yet."

"So why are you letting me out?" Grimlock asked. "Are you going to get into trouble?"

"I would NEVER do anything illegal!" Strongarm replied, glaring at him angrily.

"So why are you whispering?" Grimlock asked as he hopped out of the stasis pod. He looked around. It was night and the scrapyard was quiet. "And where are the others?"

"Shh, keep your voice down," Strongarm said. "What I'm doing is not illegal, technically. It's a loophole."

"I'm too big to fit through a loophole," Grimlock whispered.

"No, I mean I found a rule in the books that allows a law enforcement officer to release a prisoner for a period of twenty-four hours."

"Why?"

"To assist with an ongoing police enquiry."

"Will there be lots of questions?" Grimlock asked, worriedly.

"No questions," Strongarm said as patiently as she could. "You just have to help me solve the case."

"What case?!"

"Shh. The Case of the Disappearing Decepticon."

"What ... oh, you mean Hypnoscam?" Grimlock said.

"Yes," Strongarm said. "All you have to do is help me catch him."

"Can I smash him first?" Grimlock growled, remembering how the sneaky Decepticon had tricked him before. He wouldn't let that happen again!

"A little bit," Strongarm said.

"Good," Grimlock said, feeling happier now. He didn't understand all the law stuff, but smashing Decepticons he could get his head around. But then he had an awful thought.

"But what happens after we solve the case?" he asked, turning around to look at the stasis pod, now dark. "Will I have to go back in there?"

"I hope not," Strongarm said. "If we can show how useful you are in capturing Decepticons, I think it might help your appeal. Enough to make the Primes change their minds."

"Well then, what are we waiting for?" Grimlock said. He put his head back and opened his great jaws.

"No, Grimlock," Strongarm hissed. "You'll wake everyone."

But too late. Freed from the prison, Grimlock let out his pent-up frustrations

in a huge, thundering roar. Instantly, lights
turned on all around the scrapyard,
blinding them.

"Grimlock!" Strongarm said as four
figures appeared. Two Autobots and two
humans.

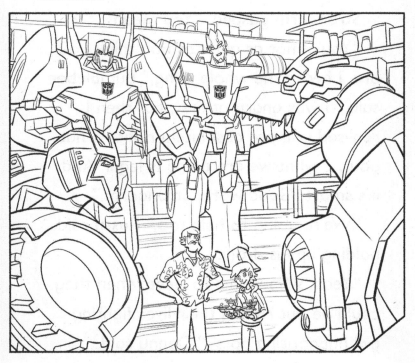

"Uh oh," Grimlock said as Bumblebee, Sideswipe, Denny and Rusty approached them. "I'm sorry, Strongarm. I guess I should get back into the stasis pod ..."

"Why would you do that?" Bumblebee said. "We have a Decepticon to catch."

Strongarm gasped. "You mean ... ?"

"You're not as quiet as you think you are. I heard the whole thing," Bumblebee said. "I was angry at first, but then I realised you are absolutely right. What you ... what we are doing is legal. And it's smart. Good work, Strongarm."

"We're going to help too," Rusty said, holding up his drone.

"Yeah, who wants to sleep when they could be out risking their lives fighting evil hypnotising bots?" Denny said.

"And if we catch the Decepticon quickly, then there'll be time to smash up the cars in my scrap pile."

"Sounds good to me," Grimlock said. He looked up into the night sky and roared again. And this time, no one tried to stop him.

CHAPTER EIGHT

"WE LAST SAW HYPNOSCAM around here," Rusty said, pointing at his tablet. He and Denny were in Strongarm's cab. Grimlock was on Strongarm's trailer, covered with a tarpaulin once more. They were racing back into Crown City, following the drone. "But where is he now?"

"I'm guessing he needed to repair himself," Bumblebee said over the radio. "He'll be looking for a big building to hide in, like ... a warehouse, maybe."

"You mean like this one?" Rusty said, zooming in on a location on the tablet. Rusty's tablet was jacked into the communicator so they could all see what was on his screen. It showed a long, tall warehouse with large hangar doors.

"Exactly like that one," Bumblebee said. "Let's check it out."

The Autobots raced to the warehouse and screeched to a stop at the main gate, where a security guard sat in a booth.

"Err, hi there," Denny said. "I'm a cop. Plain Clothes Division."

"Me too," Rusty added. "Err ... Junior Cop Division."

But the guard didn't respond. He just sat there, staring straight ahead.

"So ... yeah, we're just going to go in and check out the ... err, situation," Denny went on.

Still, the guard didn't respond. Denny and Rusty looked at each other and shrugged. Strongarm carried on cautiously, followed by Bumblebee. Sideswipe brought up the rear. They drove up to the hangar doors. Denny hopped out of the cab, looked around nervously, then walked up to the huge sliding doors and with difficulty, dragged one of them open. It was dark inside and Bumblebee nosed his way in first, waiting for his eyes to adjust to the light. What he saw made him gasp in surprise.

Humans. Dozens of them, but they weren't acting normally. They marched back and forth in teams of six, silently carrying boxes, pieces of machinery or large tools.

Beyond them, at the far end of the warehouse, Bumblebee saw Hypnoscam, in helicopter form, half covered by sheets of camouflage material. More teams of humans swarmed around him, painting and polishing. Bumblebee saw the flash of a welding torch as a human mechanic repaired some part of the Decepticon.

One of the human teams passed close by. Strongarm shone her spotlight on them but they didn't respond, they just walked on by, eyes blank.

"They're hypnotised," Sideswipe whispered as he drove up beside Bumblebee. "Hypnoscam can control humans as well as bots!"

"Then I guess we don't need to remain in disguise," Strongarm suggested. "Those humans haven't even noticed us."

"Good point," Bumblebee said. "Autobots, transform!"

With a quick crunching sound, the three vehicles transformed into bot form, standing tall. Grimlock threw the tarpaulin off and leapt from the trailer, landing with a heavy thud on the concrete floor.

Hypnoscam noticed them at this point and transformed himself into his bot form, the surrounding humans scattered, then formed themselves back into teams of six. Each human carried a weapon of some kind, whether it was a crowbar, a claw hammer or a baseball bat.

"He's made a human army," Sideswipe muttered.

"Attack!" Hypnoscam screamed, and the humans came rushing towards the bots, brandishing their weapons.

"We mustn't hurt them!" Bumblebee cried as the Autobots found themselves surrounded. "Try to disarm them without injury." The blank-faced humans ran at the Autobots, showing no fear, hitting with whatever weapons they had to hand. Denny and Rusty leapt on one worker and wrestled his crowbar away.

Strongarm made use of her riot-control training and seized a number of human attackers, plucking their weapons from their hands.

Grimlock was confused. He wanted to

smash, but understood that the humans weren't made of hard metal like Decepticons. If you hurt them, they couldn't be easily repaired. So even though it was difficult, he backed away, drawing the attackers away from the others and soaking up the blows with his tough metal plating.

Then Sideswipe and Bumblebee came rushing up, each holding a corner of the tarpaulin which had hidden Grimlock. They swept it over the large group of humans who were attacking Grimlock and gathered them up safely.

"Denny, bring those ropes over," Sideswipe cried, nodding towards a rack on the nearby wall. Quickly, Denny and Rusty encircled the struggling humans with long ropes, wrapping them up like a Christmas present.

"Useless humans," Hypnoscam spat. "No mind, I shall find myself some new slaves." He stood tall and began twirling his blades. His eyes pulsed softly, drawing the Autobots in.

"Leaks ... likes ... lights," Fixit said, staring at the Decepticon.

"Don't look at him!" Grimlock cried, lumbering in between Fixit and Hypnoscam to block the small bot's view. "That's how he gets you."

Just then, they were lit by a blinding ray of sunlight as the sliding door to the warehouse opened. A huge figure stood in the doorway. It was covered in dark, spiky armour and wore a flowing cape.

Its red eyes flashed angrily as it stepped into the hangar. Grimlock blinked against the light, trying to make out who it was.

"Liege Maximo!" Bumblebee cried. "What are you doing here?"

The Prime stormed towards them, eyes flashing with anger. "You disobeyed a direct order!" he spat at Bumblebee before pointing at Grimlock. "This ... beast should be locked up." Grimlock's heart sank as Liege Maximo waved a hand and a stasis chamber appeared as if from nowhere.

"Err, can you yell at us later?" Sideswipe said, pointing towards Hypnoscam. "We're kind of in the middle of something." Liege Maximo looked up at Hypnoscam, noticing him for the first time. The Decepticon stood watching, whirling his rotor blades, his lights pulsing hypnotically.

"Impressive power," Hypnoscam said, looking directly at Liege Maximo. "And I can use that anger." The rotor blades sped up, becoming a blur, letting off a hypnotic hum.

"Liege Maximo! Don't look at him!" Grimlock cried. But it was too late. One glance at Liege Maximo told the story. The Prime himself was under Hypnoscam's spell.

CHAPTER NINE

"UH OH," SIDESWIPE SAID AS THE huge Prime turned to them, eyes burning with fury. Liege Maximo's cape swirled around him, revealing the deadly darts on his belt. The Prime grabbed one and flung it at Sideswipe, who had to leap to one side to avoid it.

Strongarm rushed up behind the Prime. "Sorry about this, Prime," she said, leaping on to the back of the spiky bot and bringing him to the ground. But as she twisted the larger bot's arm in a wrestling move, she felt two great hands grab her shoulders and heave her aside. She went sliding across the floor, then turned to see who her attacker had been. She gasped to see a second Liege Maximo towering over her.

Hypnoscam laughed. "You metallic morons," he cried. "You've brought me a PRIME — the most powerful of all Autobots. But there's one thing even more powerful than Liege Maximo ... TWO Liege Maximos!"

Grimlock roared and charged forward at the new Prime, thudding heavily into his chest with a loud splintering crack.

But the first Liege Maximo had by now regained his feet and with a sweep of his gun arm, knocked Grimlock away from the copy. The copy lifted his own gun and blasted Grimlock in the chest at close range. The Dinobot grunted as he was slammed back into a pile of packing crates. He looked up groggily to see both Liege Maximos pointing their guns at him, ready to finish him off!

But then a flash of yellow appeared from the side and Bumblebee came crashing into the Primes, knocking them down like dominoes.

"Two against one. That's not fair," Bumblebee cried. As the first Liege Maximo tried to regain his feet, Bumblebee gave a great roundhouse kick,

knocking him back down again.
Meanwhile Sideswipe and Strongarm
helped Grimlock back to his feet and
the four Autobots clustered together,
ready to take on the dual Primes as a
team.

But as they stood, prepared for battle,
Grimlock felt his heart sink to see each
Liege Maximo split into two, then again,
until there were eight.

"We'll never be able to fight them all,"
Sideswipe said.

"We have no choice," Bumblebee
replied. "We can't leave Hypnoscam in
control of Liege Maximo. With his power,
there's no knowing what he could do."

But then the Autobots had to scatter
as the eight copies of Liege Maximo

began hurling deadly darts towards them.

"I'm hit!" Strongarm cried. Bumblebee knew this was bad news. Liege's darts were filled with poison, which would make Strongarm's joints seize up, and fast.

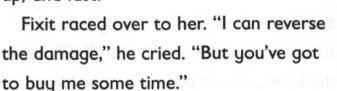

Fixit raced over to her. "I can reverse the damage," he cried. "But you've got to buy me some time."

"Leave that to me," Grimlock said, grimly. "First I got woken up, then left behind, then I got bashed, then hypnotised, then I got locked up, then I got bashed again. And I still haven't had anything to eat. I've had the worst day and my head hurts and someone's going to get SMASHED."

"You know what?" Sideswipe said to Bumblebee. "It's been ages since we went bowling."

Grimlock grinned. He knew just what to do. He rolled himself up into a ball. Sideswipe and Bumblebee took hold of him and hurled him towards the assembled Primes. The heavy ball of steel that was Grimlock SMASHED into the lead Liege Maximo, sending him pinging into the others, scattering them like bowling pins.

Then the real fight began. While Fixit worked on Strongarm, with help from

Denny and Rusty, Bumblebee, Grimlock
and Sideswipe battled against
overwhelming odds. Grimlock took on
four of the Primes himself, keeping them
at bay with great sweeps of his tail, then
rushing in to chomp with his huge jaws.
CHOMP!

Sideswipe fought like a demon, full of
whirlwind energy, battling against two of
the stronger bots, hitting them with a
furious storm of blows and kicks. SMASH!
By staying close to his opponents, he
made sure they couldn't use their lethal
darts, which were made for throwing at
enemies far away.

Bumblebee was slower and more
cautious, ducking and rolling away from
the joint attack of two Primes. He hit out

rarely, when he could see an opening, and when it really counted. All his strength, skill and experience went into the fight.

Rusty's voice came over the radio. "Bumblebee, look at Hypnoscam." Bumblebee somersaulted backwards to give himself a moment to glance over at the Decepticon. He saw Hypnoscam was sagging, supporting himself on a gantry, his blades spinning more furiously than ever and his eyes glowing dimly.

"He's tired," Rusty said. "Keeping multiple copies of a bot as powerful as Liege Maximo is taking it out of him."

"This is hopeless," Sideswipe grunted as he took a blow to the jaw from one of the copies. "There are just too many of them to contend with."

"Too many?" Bumblebee said as he ducked under a swinging fist. "Actually, our problem is that there aren't enough! We need more Liege Maximos."

"MORE?" Sideswipe cried.

"Trust me," Bumblebee said. "Everyone, scatter! We need to split them up."

The Autobots didn't need telling twice. Strongarm struggled to her feet and readied herself. Fixit raced across in front of a couple of Liege Maximos, who turned and followed him across the warehouse, flinging darts as they went.

Denny and Rusty ran left and right, throwing spanners and hammers at the Primes, drawing their attention. Bumblebee, Grimlock and Sideswipe spread out, each taking two of the Primes with them.

Hypnoscam roared in frustration. His forces were being spread thinly.

With a popping sound, eight more Liege Maximos appeared. Hypnoscam slumped to his knees.

"Sixteen!" Sideswipe cried, backing away as more Primes rushed to attack. "Bumblebee, we have to get out of here!"

"Wait," Bumblebee replied as Grimlock sent two of the new copies scattering with a well-aimed flick of his tail. "The more copies there are, the weaker they become." To prove his point, he punched the closest Liege Maximo in the chest.

BAM! The copy flew backwards and slammed into a steel wall, leaving a huge dent, before sliding down to the floor in a tangle of spiky limbs.

"In that case," Sideswipe said, "it's crunching time!" He took a couple of running steps and launched himself, feet first, at the nearest adversary. His legs hit the larger bot with a satisfying SMASH, sending him soaring into a pile of packing crates.

From that point, the battle got a lot easier. Copies of Liege Maximo were sent flying left, right and centre. "That's for sending my buddy into stasis," Sideswipe said as he crunched one copy of the Prime underfoot.

"Grimlock," Bumblebee cried as the battle raged. "Hypnoscam is distracted. You know what that means."

"I sure do," Grimlock replied, his eyes flashing. "It's smashing time!"

CHAPTER TEN

GRIMLOCK CHARGED AT Hypnoscam, who looked up and scrambled to his feet when he realised the danger he was in. Hypnoscam's eyes flashed and his rotor blades whirled as he tried to put Grimlock under hypnosis.

But too late.

"Not THIS time!" Grimlock roared and the Dinobot bashed into Hypnoscam, sending him flying. CRUNCH! The smaller bot landed in a heap of tangled limbs and bent rotor blades. Grimlock leapt into the air and came crashing down on top of the smaller bot, pinning him to the floor until the others arrived.

Strongarm dragged the stasis chamber up and they bundled the dazed Hypnoscam inside without ceremony.

"Liege Maximo, are you OK?" Denny asked. They turned to see the spiky Prime climbing unsteadily to his feet. He stared around, confused, as his copies vanished one by one. Under the tarpaulin, they heard the humans begin to awaken from their hypnosis and struggle to get free. Hypnoscam's spell was broken.

"I think we'd better get everyone back to the scrapyard," Bumblebee said, "before those humans see us. Grimlock, you'll have to squeeze on to the trailer with the stasis chamber."

Working quickly, Strongarm and

Sideswipe lifted the stasis chamber on to the trailer, then covered it and Grimlock with another tarpaulin they'd found in a storeroom.

"I'm sorry, Liege Maximo, but we can't allow you to be seen," Bumblebee said. "It'll be tight, but we could squeeze you on to Strongarm's trailer as well."

"I can provide my own transportation," the Prime said, coldly. He waved a hand and a groundbridge opened up with a dazzling display of coloured light. Through the portal Bumblebee could see the scrapyard. Liege Maximo stepped through and the groundbridge closed behind him.

"Well, that was rude," Sideswipe said. "He could have taken us with him."

"We don't need a groundbridge," Bumblebee said. "Come on, Autobots, rev up and roll out!"

They pulled out of the warehouse and passed the puzzled-looking guard on the gate.

"Thanks," Rusty said to him as they drove by. "Everything seems to be in order."

They drove slowly this time, trying not to attract attention. As they passed the doughnut factory Grimlock saw a team of workers lifting a new giant doughnut to the roof. His stomach growled.

Dawn was breaking as they drove back through the forest. Grimlock breathed in the fresh air, smelling pine trees. He didn't want to go back into that stasis chamber. He wanted to be free to charge through the forest, being careful not to knock any trees over, of course. He wanted to crunch cars in the scrapyard. He wanted to play hide-and-seek with his friends. But most of all, he wanted to eat a massive metal doughnut.

Back at the scrapyard, Grimlock crept away to hide, fearful that Liege Maximo would insist he was returned to stasis. Liege Maximo addressed Bumblebee. He seemed to be finding it difficult to get the words out.

"I feel I must thank you for ... dealing with the Decepticon," the Prime said, quietly, not meeting Bumblebee's eye.

"And for releasing you from his hypnotic spell," Sideswipe added. "Don't forget that bit."

Liege Maximo flushed. "I admit I felt momentarily ... confused."

"It's not me you should thank," Bumblebee said. "It's Grimlock. The Dinobot you want to put into stasis."

Liege Maximo looked furious.

"Luckily for you, Grimlock had been released from the stasis chamber to assist with capturing the Decepticon," Strongarm added. "All within the rules, of course."

"Yes, well. Rules ARE important," Liege Maximo said. "And that's why ..."

"... And if we're sticking to the rules," Strongarm continued, "then any bot must be sent into stasis if they attack other Autobots. Even a Prime."

"Even if they were under hypnosis at the time," Rusty added, nodding seriously. Sideswipe, Strongarm and

Bumblebee all stared at Liege Maximo.

"Rules are rules," Sideswipe said.

"So," Bumblebee said. "If you feel you must punish Grimlock, then that's understandable, but you must also punish yourself. That's only fair."

"And there's a spare stasis chamber in the barn," Denny added. "Just about your size, Liege Maximo."

Liege Maximo's eyes flashed in anger. He knew he was defeated.

"Well ..." Liege Maximo stammered. "I think ... in my judgement as one of the Thirteen Primes ... that in light of the exemplary service the Dinobot performed ... that a pardon can be arranged."

"Is that a thank you?" Bumblebee asked the Prime.

"Don't push me, Bumblebee," Liege Maximo snapped. "I am willing to overlook Grimlock's transgression on this occasion, on one condition."

"What's that?" Bumblebee asked.

"That this … episode … isn't reported to the other Primes."

"I think we can agree to that," Bumblebee said.

"Good," Liege Maximo said, then without so much as a goodbye, he turned and stepped forward as one end of a groundbridge appeared in thin air, dazzling them all with its brightness. Liege Maximo stepped into it, disappearing from view. The rip closed behind him as if it had never been there.

"Is it ... is it safe to come out now?" Grimlock asked, from behind a mountain of cars.

"It sure is!" Bumblebee cried. The others surrounded the Dinobot, slapping him on the back. Rusty wrapped his arms around one of Grimlock's great legs and squeezed it tight.

"It's good to have you back," Strongarm said.

"It was much too quiet around here without you," Sideswipe agreed. "And I had no one to wrestle with."

Grimlock laughed and whipped his tail around, knocking Sideswipe to the dusty ground again.

"That's more like it," Sideswipe coughed.

"This calls for a party," Denny said.

"A party?" Grimlock asked.

"The biggest, loudest party ever," Denny cried, pointing to the huge pile of wrecks Grimlock had been hiding behind.

"A SMASHING party."

"I hope you're hungry," Rusty said as Grimlock chomped his great jaws in anticipation.

"Always, Rusty," Grimlock roared happily. He was home, with his friends and it a big pile of metal. It was time to SMASH!

· · · MISSION COMPLETE · · ·

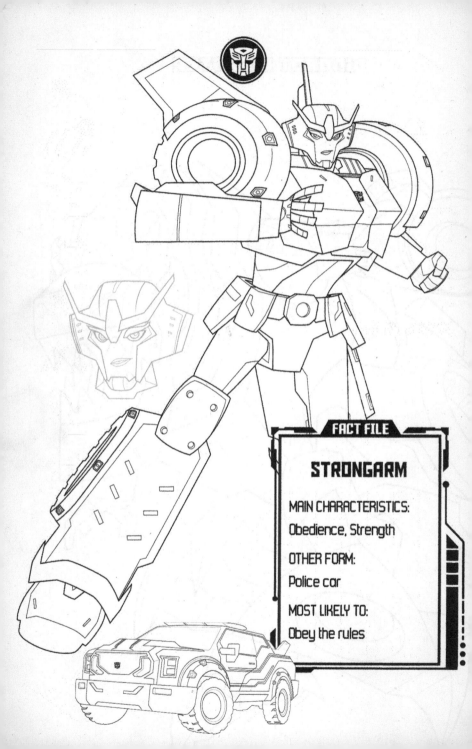

FACT FILE

STRONGARM

MAIN CHARACTERISTICS:
Obedience, Strength

OTHER FORM:
Police car

MOST LIKELY TO:
Obey the rules

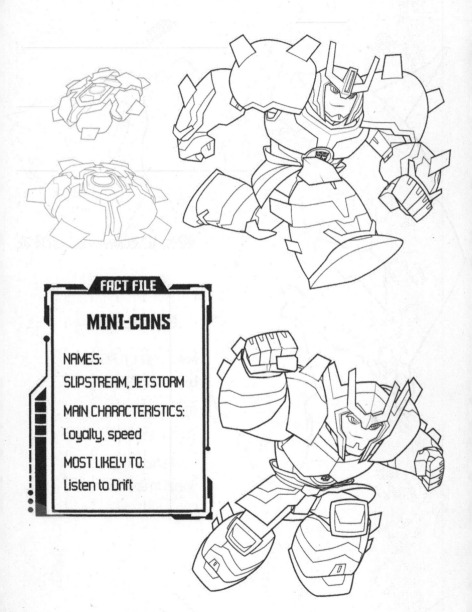

MINI-CONS

NAMES:
SLIPSTREAM, JETSTORM

MAIN CHARACTERISTICS:
Loyalty, speed

MOST LIKELY TO:
Listen to Drift

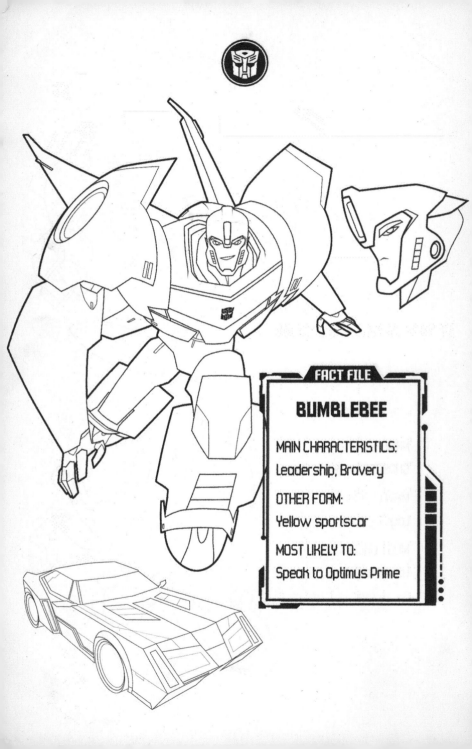

FACT FILE

BUMBLEBEE

MAIN CHARACTERISTICS:
Leadership, Bravery

OTHER FORM:
Yellow sportscar

MOST LIKELY TO:
Speak to Optimus Prime

FACT FILE

SIDESWIPE

MAIN CHARACTERISTICS:
Humour, Impulsiveness

OTHER FORM:
Red sportscar

MOST LIKELY TO:
Have a race

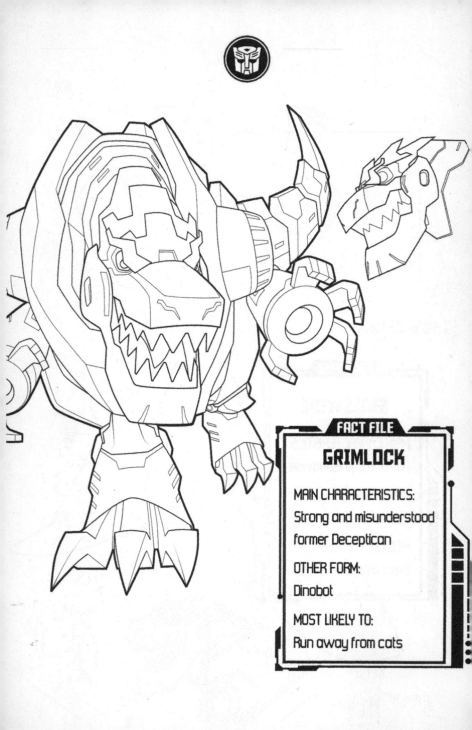

FACT FILE

GRIMLOCK

MAIN CHARACTERISTICS:
Strong and misunderstood
former Deceptican

OTHER FORM:
Dinobot

MOST LIKELY TO:
Run away from cats

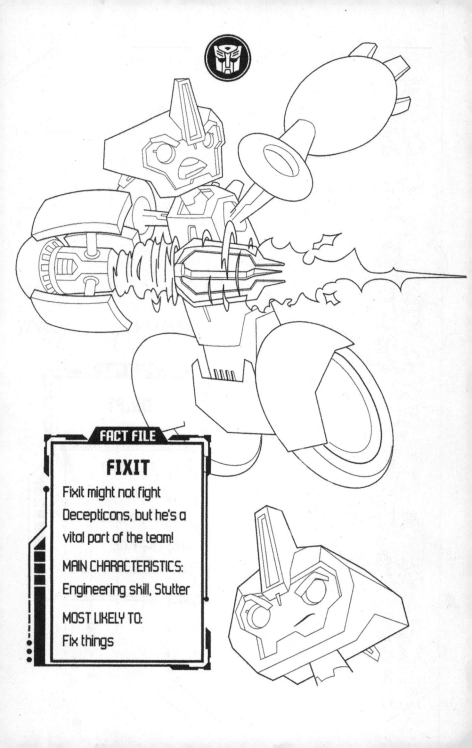

FACT FILE

FIXIT

Fixit might not fight Decepticons, but he's a vital part of the team!

MAIN CHARACTERISTICS:
Engineering skill, Stutter

MOST LIKELY TO:
Fix things

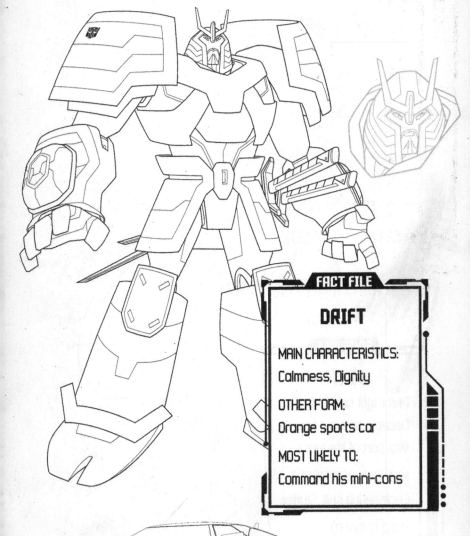

FACT FILE

DRIFT

MAIN CHARACTERISTICS:
Calmness, Dignity

OTHER FORM:
Orange sports car

MOST LIKELY TO:
Command his mini-cons